VIEW TO A GRILL

IRON & FLAME COZY MYSTERIES, BOOK 3

PATTI BENNING

SUMMER PRESCOTT BOOKS PUBLISHING

Copyright 2024 Summer Prescott Books

All Rights Reserved. No part of this publication nor any of the information herein may be quoted from, nor reproduced, in any form, including but not limited to: printing, scanning, photocopying, or any other printed, digital, or audio formats, without prior express written consent of the copyright holder.

**This book is a work of fiction. Any similarities to persons, living or dead, places of business, or situations past or present, is completely unintentional.

ONE

"There you are!"

Lydia Thackery finished locking her car, then glanced over her shoulder to see Valerie Morale waving at her from across the street on the sidewalk in front of Morning Dove. The cafe had a sign with a stylized dove drinking coffee on it, there was a nest in the gutter that held a pair of pigeons in the warmer months, though she didn't think that was by design. It was a lovely place to get a meal or cup of coffee at, but normally Lydia preferred to visit it *after* the sun rose. With a morose look up at the dark sky, she crossed the street and joined her friend.

"I'm glad I'm not the first one here," she said. "I was a little worried everyone else was going to bail, and I would have woken up at five-thirty in the morning for nothing."

"You're actually the last one here," Valerie said as she pulled the door open. "None of us have been here long, though."

Warm air and the scent of coffee and frying bacon wrapped around Lydia, and she gladly stepped inside out of the cold darkness of the winter morning. Sure enough, she spotted Taylor and Sierra, the other two friends she was meeting here, seated at one of the corner tables.

Lydia and Valerie joined them. No one had coffee yet, which meant Valerie had probably been telling the truth about them not waiting long. Setting her purse down on the floor between her feet — the booths were a little crowded with all four of them and their winter coats — she exchanged a round of greetings with the other women.

"Isn't this nice?" Taylor asked. "Quarry Creek is so peaceful in the mornings."

"I could do with better scenery," Sierra muttered.

Lydia followed the other woman's glance toward a booth along the back wall. A woman was sitting at it.

Her back was to them, but when she turned her head to glance toward the counter, Lydia realized she recognized her. Mariah Bancroft.

"Yeah, she just got here a minute or two after I did," Taylor whispered. "What a coincidence, right? But we shouldn't let her chase us out of here."

"I don't understand," Valerie murmured, leaning forward. "Who is she, and why do all of you hate her?"

Valerie was new to their friend group—Lydia had met her at Iron and Flame a couple of months ago, and they had hit it off. When she reconnected with Taylor and the others, she had introduced Valerie to them as well. They all got along, and it was nice to know that their group was growing instead of shrinking.

Taylor and Sierra exchanged glances. Sierra crossed her arms, but gave a brief nod, giving Taylor permission to explain.

"Sierra was engaged a couple years ago," Taylor said. "Up until she found out Mariah was having an affair with her fiancé."

Valerie winced. "That's terrible. Did she know you were seeing him?"

Sierra gave a bitter laugh. "Oh, she knew. She used to be one of my closest friends."

"As soon as we found out what happened, we all dropped her as a friend," Lydia added. She had still been involved with the group when all of this happened and remembered it clearly. Even though Mariah hadn't done anything to her, she had felt the same sense of betrayal as the others had. "I don't think any of us could have trusted her after that."

"Oh, wow. I don't blame you; I don't think I would be able to trust a friend who did that either."

Valerie gave the other woman a narrow-eyed look, and Sierra and Taylor both looked angry. Lydia had a feeling that if she didn't change the subject soon, their breakfast was going to start off on a bad note.

Before she could come up with something that was both cheerful enough and distracting enough to remove the subject of Mariah from their minds entirely, the door to the kitchen opened and the owner of Morning Dove, a woman about Lydia's age named Cynthia Dutton, came out. She spotted their full table and hurried over, bringing a pot of coffee and a stack of menus with her.

"I'm so sorry for the wait," she said as she set the menus down and started pouring coffee into their mugs. "We're down an employee unexpectedly, and I'm here by myself this morning. I've been in a rush to get everything going in the kitchen. What can I get for you ladies today? Or do you want to look at the menu first?"

All of them came here often enough that they already knew what they wanted. Lydia ordered the crepes with a cinnamon apple crumble filling. They were a far cry from real French crepes, but they were still pretty good, and any morning when she was out of bed before the sun was up, she intended to treat herself.

Cynthia didn't bother writing any of their orders down, and since Lydia had never gotten the wrong food when she came here, she was impressed rather than worried. She needed to write every detail down if she took so much as one person's order.

While Cynthia walked over to Mariah's table to take her order and pour her coffee, Valerie reached for the little dish of coffee creamer and poured a couple into her mug before stirring it. Lydia reached for the sugar, idly sorting through the packets. There was only one packet of real sugar, and she was about to see if she could get Cynthia's attention to ask for more, but before she could say something, the other woman reentered the kitchen.

At her booth, Mariah got up and headed toward the restroom. Sierra was purposefully not looking at her. Lydia was glad, not for the first time, that her own divorce with Jeremy had been relatively drama free. She did not envy her friend in the slightest.

"Ugh, this coffee tastes weird," Valerie said.

Lydia tasted hers. It was black and bitter when it touched her tongue, but it didn't seem off.

"It tastes normal to me."

"All of the creamer in this bowl says it's real dairy," Taylor said, examining the little cups. "I'm pretty sure they're supposed to be refrigerated. They're probably spoiled. I'll go grab another bowl from one of the other tables. You can ask Cynthia for some more coffee when she gets back with our food."

"You should switch it with the creamer on Mariah's table," Sierra muttered darkly. "If anyone deserves coffee that tastes like spoiled milk, it's her."

Taylor smirked; a smug, mean expression that made Lydia uncomfortable. Kicking Mariah out of their friend group was one thing, and something she had completely supported given the circumstances. This seemed petty and too close to bullying for her tastes.

But Sierra was the one who had been forced to deal with a cheating fiancé and a horrible betrayal from one of her best friends all at the same time, so she kept her mouth shut as Taylor got up and carried the little ceramic bowl of bad creamers over to Mariah's table. She made the switch and came back, putting the new bowl with a variety of non-dairy creamers down on their table.

Lydia still needed to finish fixing up her coffee, so she dumped the sugar packet in and grabbed one of the new creamers. Hopefully, Mariah drank her coffee black or only with sugar. She wouldn't say Mariah didn't deserve some bad luck, but she still felt a little guilty for not saying anything.

"So, why did you want to meet here so early?" Sierra asked after the soft clinking of their spoons as they stirred their coffees faded. "It's cold and dark outside, and I want a good reason for having gotten out of bed."

Taylor, who was the one who had begged them all to meet here right when the cafe opened, sighed and put the spoon she had used to stir her coffee down. "I know none of you wanted to get up this early, but I also knew we were all going to be busy with work today and there's something I wanted to get off my chest. Martin and I are getting a divorce."

Lydia blinked, then stared at her friend. Even Valerie, who hadn't known Taylor for very long, looked shocked. Sierra just looked flabbergasted.

"What?" Lydia asked. "But you said the two of you were doing fine just a couple weeks ago. What happened?"

"I know it's sudden," Taylor said. "I was actually hoping you could help me with something. Your sister is still a paralegal, right? Can you put me in touch with her?"

The bathroom door opened, and Lydia glanced over distractedly as Mariah came out of the bathroom and sat back down at her table. She didn't seem to notice that the bowl of creamers had been switched, and Lydia winced as she saw the other woman dump one of the little plastic containers into her coffee and stir it.

"Yeah, she's still working at the law firm," she said, forcing her attention back to the conversation. "But if you're looking for a good divorce lawyer, I can recommend the woman who helped me. Her price was fair, or at least I thought so, and she was quite helpful. She explained how everything worked and was just really easy to get along with."

"I'd appreciate that," Taylor said. "I still can't believe this is happening to me. I mean, when you and Jeremy split up, it was surprising enough, but I always thought Martin and I were forever, you know?"

Lydia did know. She knew the statistics for divorce, of course, but just like Taylor, she had never thought it would happen to her.

"I'm no longer annoyed that you made us meet you here this early," Sierra said somberly. "This must be so hard for you. Are you still staying at your house?"

As Taylor nodded, Lydia heard a clatter and turned to see Mariah had dropped her silverware on the floor. Valerie glanced over at her too, but quickly returned her attention to the conversation. Lydia frowned when she saw Mariah start itching her neck instead of reaching for the silverware. When the other woman turned her head, she spotted a flush of red on her face. After a moment, Mariah got up and rushed to the restroom.

No one else seemed to notice. Sierra and Valerie were staring at Taylor, who was talking about how they had already agreed that she would get the house.

"Well, he said he wasn't going to fight for it, but who really knows how things will turn out. I'm dreading all of the legal stuff."

"I'll be here to help if you need advice or even just someone who knows what you're going through to complain to," Lydia said. "It's not fun, and I won't sugarcoat it, but it's doable. And once you're done, you're going to feel such a weight lift off of you."

Taylor gave her a shaky smile. "Thanks. I knew I could count on you guys. I feel less alone already."

The door to the kitchen opened, and they all looked around as Cynthia came out, a platter of food balanced on one hand. She smiled as she carried it over and started setting their plates down in front of them.

"Here you go, ladies. Let me know if you need anything else. Don't hesitate to poke your head into the kitchen to get my attention. Like I said, I'm the only one working here this morning, so there won't be anyone else coming out to do the rounds."

In the brief silence that fell at the end of her sentence before they could thank her, something loud thudded against the bathroom door. They all turned to look at it.

"Is everything all right in there?" Cynthia called out. There was no answer. Giving them a tight, concerned smile, she grabbed the tray and walked toward the bathroom. The others were already digging into their food, but Lydia had a niggling feeling that something was wrong, and she watched as Cynthia opened the bathroom door. She stepped inside, and the door swung shut behind her.

A moment later, she screamed.

TWO

Valerie jolted so hard she knocked her coffee mug to the floor, where it shattered, sending hot coffee everywhere. Sierra gave a yelp of alarm, and Taylor dropped her fork. Lydia just sat up straighter and gave a sharp gasp of surprise. The bathroom door opened, and Cynthia looked out at them, her eyes wide and panicked.

"Hurry, someone check her purse and see if she has an EpiPen."

There was a moment of stunned stillness at their table before Lydia started moving. She nudged Valerie, who needed to get out of the booth before she could, and that was enough to get the rest of them scrambling to their feet. They hurried over to

Mariah's table. Taylor reached for the other woman's purse, but as she turned, the shoulder strap caught on the corner of the table and yanked it out of her hands. The purse turned upside down as it fell, and when it hit the floor, its contents spilled out in a mess.

Taylor shoved some of the mess aside so she could crouch down next to the booth, and Valerie crouched opposite her as she began to dig through the items. Sierra hovered over them, wringing her hands. Lydia decided not to crowd in beside her.

"I can't find one!" Valerie said after a few frantic seconds of searching.

"Do you know what you're looking for?" Taylor asked.

"Yes, my brother is allergic to shellfish, and he's had one since he was ten."

"Hurry up," Cynthia screamed from the bathroom. "I don't think she's breathing!"

"We can't find one!" Taylor shouted back.

"Then call an ambulance!"

Lydia turned back to the table, intending to find her phone, but Sierra had hers in her hand already and said, "I'll do it. I need to do something useful."

While Sierra dialed the number, Lydia decided to make herself useful as well, and hurried to the bathroom to see what was going on. She pulled the door open and saw Cynthia kneeling on the ground next to Mariah, who was lying too still on her back. She had hives all over her face, her neck, and what Lydia could see of her hands and arms.

"Can you help me?" Cynthia asked, her voice frantic. "She isn't breathing. We need to do something."

Lydia crouched by Mariah's head and tried to tilt it up, not sure if it was helping or not. She wracked her mind, trying to figure out what had happened. She vaguely remembered Mariah having an allergy, but she couldn't remember what it was to. She should know this—as a chef, she was always very careful about people's allergies, but it had been years since she'd spoken to Mariah, or even thought of her very much.

"Did she mention any allergies when she ordered her food?" Lydia asked.

"She said she has a sesame allergy, but I hadn't even gotten the food out to her yet, so I don't see how it could be something she ate."

"Could there have been cross-contamination with something on her silverware or in her coffee mug or the coffee pot?"

"It's not like I wash my dishes in sesame oil," Cynthia snapped. "Do you know CPR? I took a course, but it was years ago. Oh my gosh, can you feel her pulse?"

Lydia pressed her fingers into Mariah's neck and couldn't feel anything. She tried her wrist next, with the same result. She didn't know if she was missing it because she was panicking, or if the other woman's heart had truly stopped beating. How long had it been since they heard the thud of her collapsing against the door?

"We need to start chest compressions," Cynthia said. "Here, move aside, I'll do it."

Feeling useless, Lydia moved to the side as Cynthia started trying to do chest compressions on the other woman. She wasn't any help here, so she rose to her feet, wondering if she could find an EpiPen anywhere else—surely someone in the surrounding area had one, and if she had to start waving down cars and asking, she would do it.

"The ambulance is going to be here soon," Sierra called from the dining area.

Lydia shoved the bathroom door open and went on her tiptoes to set the lock on the hinge so it wouldn't swing shut again. They needed to be able to communicate, and she didn't want the door to get in the way of the paramedics.

"They need to get here now," she said.

"I don't think they can hurry any faster," Sierra retorted. "The dispatcher wants to know if she's breathing."

Before Lydia could answer, Valerie, who had been on her hands and knees under the booth, stood up triumphantly, something clenched in her hand. "I found it! Someone must have kicked it under the table when the purse spilled."

"Well, hurry!" Lydia said, stepping back to clear the doorway. "She needs it now!"

Valerie rushed into the bathroom and knelt by Cynthia, who was still trying to do chest compressions on Mariah. Lydia felt the other two women crowd around her as they all peered through the bathroom door together. Valerie took the cap off of the EpiPen and injected it into Mariah's thigh.

There was a hush as they waited for a response, but as the seconds ticked by and nothing happened, Lydia began to understand that they were too late. In all of the time they had spent panicking and making things worse, the allergic reaction had closed off Mariah's throat, and she had stopped breathing. She didn't know how many minutes had passed since then, but it had been too long.

The wailing of the ambulance siren started on the edges of their hearing, getting louder and louder with each passing second, but none of them could tear their eyes away from Mariah where she lay on the bathroom floor.

THREE

Lydia didn't think the people of Quarry Creek had ever seen a tragedy quite so early in the morning. The sky was just beginning to lighten with dawn as the ambulance pulled out of Morning Dove's parking lot. The sirens and flashing lights had caught the attention of passersby on their way to work and school, and the street was unusually crowded for such an early hour.

She stood on the sidewalk and watched as the ambulance pulled away. The entire morning felt unreal. She wished she could believe it was all just a bad dream, and that she would wake up in a few hours to find that none of this had happened. She might not have liked Mariah much, but there was a big difference between thinking someone was a terrible person and wanting them dead.

"I can't believe it," Sierra muttered. "It all happened so fast."

"I hope Cynthia doesn't get in trouble for this," Taylor said softly, glancing back over her shoulder.

Lydia followed her gaze and saw Cynthia talking with the police in front of the cafe. The responding officers had already spoken to the four of them, and there hadn't been much to say. They had been sitting at their own table, across the room from Mariah, who they hadn't said a single word to, when she suddenly started scratching at herself and ran into the bathroom. The only one still alive who could possibly know what had happened was Cynthia, and she had remained adamant that there was no way anything sesame related could have contaminated something at Mariah's table.

"Maybe there was a sesame seed stuck to the booth somewhere," Valerie suggested. "She said it was a busy morning. Maybe she didn't have time to wipe the booths down like normal."

"Do you think she could get in legal trouble for that?" Sierra asked, biting her lip as the four of them watched the other woman.

Cynthia was a complete mess, just on this side of hysterical. Lydia didn't blame her—she had watched a customer die in front of her. Her heart ached for the other woman. She couldn't imagine how guilty she would feel if something similar happened at Iron and Flame.

"She will probably face some liability for it, depending on what the police find as the cause of her death," Lydia said. "I feel really bad for her."

"So, if she did it, do you think that means Morning Dove is going to close down?" Taylor asked.

"Maybe," Lydia said. "I don't know what sort of legal consequences she might face, exactly. She might get sued, if Mariah's family decides to pursue legal action. She might be forced to sell the business to pay the fees, if she does." She frowned. "Though, when you say *if she did it,* it makes it sound like she killed Mariah on purpose. I'm sure whatever happened was just an accident. A horrible, horrible accident."

"Maybe she *did* do it on purpose," Sierra muttered. "Who knows who else Mariah's been sleeping with. I doubt my relationship is the only one she's ever wrecked."

"Well, Cynthia isn't married," Valerie said. "We talk sometimes, when I stop in to grab takeout. I don't think she was even dating anyone."

"Yeah, we shouldn't make more out of this than there is," Taylor said. "There's a big difference between someone being a little careless in the kitchen and straight up murder."

"I just wish we could have done more," Lydia said with a sigh. "We all panicked, and I'm not saying it was anyone's fault, but we just made things worse."

"Well, I'm not going to let it eat me up," Sierra said briskly. Reaching into her purse, she took out her car keys. "It couldn't have happened to a better person, as far as I'm concerned. The police said they're done with us, so I'm going to head out. I'll see you ladies later. Taylor, give me a call when you have time. I want to hear more about you and Martin."

They all said goodbye to Sierra. As she walked away to her car, Lydia turned to Taylor. "I'm here to talk if you need me too. Give me a call anytime. I won't be able to talk if I'm at work, but I'll call you back when I can."

"Same," Valerie said. "I know we don't know each other very well, but I'm always here if you need a shoulder to cry on."

"Thanks," Taylor said. "And thanks for meeting me here so early, I really appreciate it. I'm sorry things turned out so badly."

Lydia assured her it wasn't her fault, and with a last wave goodbye, Taylor left. Valerie paused long enough to say goodbye to Lydia, then headed home as well. That left her standing alone on the sidewalk. She glanced back toward Morning Dove, but the police were still talking to Cynthia. Iron and Flame was kitty-corner across the street, but it was still hours until she needed to open it, so she decided to just head home.

With a little luck, there would be enough time for her to straighten out her thoughts so she would be on top of her game by the time she opened the restaurant.

When she got to Iron and Flame at ten, she was still shaken up by what had happened to Mariah, but now that she'd had time to dwell on it, what had shaken her even more was the reminder of how easily a mistake like that could happen in even the best kitchen. No matter what happened with the legal side of things, she knew Cynthia was never going to forgive herself for today. Even if it had been a freak occurrence, something anyone could have missed, she knew the other woman was going to blame herself. Lydia would have, if she was in her shoes.

As a chef, her responsibility wasn't just to make delicious food. It was to make *safe* food. She took that responsibility seriously, which was reflected by the policies in their kitchen. They were very careful with cross-contamination. They had a separate area they used to prepare and cook their gluten free buns and breadsticks, separate pots and pans they used for the most common allergens, a griddle that they never cooked seafood on, and a laminated guide to the most common allergens and the foods they were in. If any one of the servers was unsure whether the kitchen could accommodate an allergen request, they were supposed to bring the request back to whoever the head chef on shift was, and if they weren't one hundred percent sure they could serve the guests a safe meal, they would let the guest know and politely refuse to serve them.

They didn't mess around. They had never dealt with a major incident so far, but she knew the events of today would stay with her for a long, long time.

When she opened the kitchen that morning, she took their allergen guide down off the wall and poured over it, wondering if she could improve it. She wished there was a way to know for sure what had happened to Mariah. If it was something Cynthia hadn't thought of, it might be something she and Jeremy hadn't thought of either. While Morning Dove might not be a fine dining establishment, she had a lot of respect for the other woman and had always been comfortable eating in Cynthia's restaurant—which she couldn't say for every restaurant she had visited. She didn't think Cynthia would have made an obvious mistake, and she didn't like not knowing what had happened. She didn't like thinking it might be a mistake she could make as well.

She would just have to follow the news about Mariah's death and wait and see if any solid answers ever came out. In the meantime, she would be extra careful. She decided to give her employees a brief talk about what happened to remind them how seriously they had to take every allergy they came across.

What happened to Mariah earlier that morning would never happen to anyone in her restaurant. She was going to make sure of it.

FOUR

The tragedy kept her mood low for the rest of the week. She had the weekend off, and when she woke up on Saturday morning, she felt a guilty sense of relief that she had two days in a row where she didn't have to worry about accidentally killing someone who had an allergy. Mariah's death was haunting her, not because she had particularly liked the woman, but because of how much it terrified her to think she could make whatever simple mistake Cynthia had made and be the cause of someone's death herself.

She didn't have any major plans this weekend other than meeting Jude Holloway, a game warden she had become friends with a couple months ago, for a hike through the woods with his dog.

She had been meeting him almost every weekend, and sometimes even during the week. She hadn't dated much since her divorce—just a few half-hearted dinner dates with people she had met online, before she realized she wasn't ready for a serious relationship yet—but she couldn't deny that she liked Jude. He was kind, easygoing, and couldn't have been more different from Jeremy if he tried. For now, though, they were just friends who enjoyed each other's company, and she was hardly going to complain about that. It was good to have a reason to get outside and be active. She might be on her feet all day at work, but she didn't usually get much exercise other than that. She used to jog, but it was hard to make herself go for a run when she was exhausted from working all day. She had been trying to pick up the habit again, but it just wouldn't stick.

The hikes were a good way to get her heart rate up and her blood pumping, at least. Another upside was that Jude was a good person to bounce her thoughts off of. She had a lot on her mind, so she didn't waste any time in getting ready for their hike that afternoon. She was looking forward to seeing him, and not just because she liked being around him. She was hoping he might be able to help her feel a hair less worried about accidentally killing someone with the next steak she made.

It was a cold day, and the sky was overcast, but the weather app on her phone wasn't warning about precipitation. There was already snow on the ground, but it was a week old and starting to get dingy looking. She had beat Jude to the trail for once and took the time to pull her ice cleats on over the soles of her boots while she waited. The snow on the trail was compacted and icy from all of the people that had walked over it, and the last thing she wanted was to fall. Winter in northern Wisconsin could get brutal, and she was already sick and tired of it.

When she saw Jude pull into the parking lot in his truck, she waved and walked over to greet him and Saffron, his little yellow mutt. She was a medium-size dog with one pricked up ear and one floppy one, and she was perpetually happy. He let her out of the truck on her long leash, and Lydia greeted her first, crouching down to bury her fingers in the soft fur behind the dog's ears. She gave her a good scratch while Saffron's entire body wiggled with joy.

"Hey, sweet girl. How have you been doing? Are you looking forward to our walk today?"

In response, Saffron licked her across the face, leaving her sputtering and wiping at her lips as she stood up.

Jude chuckled. "Sorry about that. She had a boring week, so I think she's a little more hyper than she usually is."

"It's fine," Lydia said, laughing. Her heart felt lighter already. She knew pets were supposed to be good for stress, but she hadn't expected the effects to be quite so noticeable. "How are you doing? Was your week boring too?"

As they talked, they started toward the trailhead. There was only one other car in the parking lot, so she suspected they would have a nice, quiet hike today.

"For the most part. We had one issue with someone shooting a deer in his neighbor's backyard, right here in town. It's not deer season anymore, and even if it was, it would have been an illegal shot, due to the proximity of the buildings. I've been collaborating with the police on the case. It's pretty cut and dry, but it's one of those cases that just boggles my mind. I have no idea why he thought he would get away with it."

"Some people don't think the consequences of their actions through," Lydia mused.

"That's true. Oh, did you hear about what happened at Morning Dove earlier this week?"

Lydia sighed. She had been planning on bringing up Mariah's death anyway, but she had hoped for some lighter conversation first. "I did more than hear about it. I was there, eating breakfast with my friends when it happened."

He grimaced. "Oh, that's rough. I saw a post about it online the day it happened, but I was at the police station yesterday, and I heard they're treating it as a homicide."

"They're what?" she asked, stunned.

"Uh, that might not have been public knowledge. Can you pretend I didn't say anything?"

"No," she said bluntly. "I won't tell anyone else, but homicide? Are you sure?"

"A couple guys at the police station mentioned it in passing. I don't know any details. What happened, exactly? If you were there, you probably know more than I do."

As they paused to let Saffron sniff at an especially interesting clump of snow, Lydia started telling him all about the early morning disaster at Morning Dove. When she finished, his lips were pulled down into a frown of consideration.

"Why did she run into the bathroom?" he asked. "Why not reach straight for her EpiPen?"

"I don't know," Lydia said. "I hadn't even thought of that. Maybe she wasn't sure what was happening. I doubt she was expecting to have an allergic reaction to her morning cup of coffee. It's possible she might have thought something else was wrong. If she felt like she was going to get sick, her only thought might have been to make it to a toilet in time."

"Do you think she would have made it if the EpiPen was where it was supposed to be in her purse, or did too much time pass before someone found her in the bathroom?"

"I'm no medical expert, but I think she would have made it," Lydia said. "Only about thirty seconds passed between when she went down in the bathroom and when Cynthia checked on her. We all heard her fall. She might have stopped breathing by then, but I'm sure her heart was still beating. I have no idea how that EpiPen got under the booth. Even after the purse spilled, it should have been in the pile with her other things. You would think if one of us kicked it accidentally, we would have realized it."

His frown deepened. "You don't think someone kicked it out of the way on purpose, do you?"

Lydia froze. She had been thinking about what happened to Mariah a lot over the past few days. Almost constantly, in fact, especially when she was at work. But this entire time, she had been thinking it was nothing but a terrible, terrible accident.

What if she was wrong? What if someone had hidden the EpiPen on purpose?

"She used to be a part of my group of friends," Lydia said slowly. "Years ago, before Jeremy and I got divorced. I was never especially close to her, but I knew her pretty well. Sierra was the one she was closest to. They had known each other since high school. Sierra was engaged to someone who had moved here for some reason, I don't even remember why by now. Anyway, they had been dating for a couple years at that point and had been engaged for about six months. Everything was going well until Sierra found inappropriate text messages on his phone ... between him and Mariah."

Jude winced. "Ouch."

"Yeah. It was pretty clear what was going on from the text messages, but she wanted to have proof. She followed him over to Mariah's house one day when he said he was going to work early and caught him kissing her at the door. She took a picture and sent it to our group text and ... well, let's just say that I don't think there's been that much drama in our friend group before or since. She broke up with her fiancé, of course, and we all turned against Mariah immediately. Honestly, if anything, I think she was more hurt that Mariah would do that to her than that her fiancé was cheating. The betrayal hits differently coming from someone who was your best friend since high school, you know? She's hated Mariah ever since. I can't say I blame her."

"I wouldn't either. It sounds like Mariah was a terrible friend."

"Yeah, well, Sierra was pretty unhappy that she was at Morning Dove that morning. I had assumed one of us had just accidentally knocked the EpiPen aside with our shoe and somehow didn't notice, or maybe it rolled under the table on its own, but now I'm starting to wonder if she kicked it out of the way on purpose." Lydia took a deep, shaky breath before continuing. "And afterward, when we were saying goodbye before we went our separate ways, she didn't seem too concerned by what happened. A little shocked, maybe, but if anything, she seemed glad that Mariah was dead."

"Do you think she could do something like that?" he asked.

"I don't know," Lydia said quietly. "I want to say no, but if even the police think there's something else going on ... maybe I need to consider it. I think I need to go talk to her after this."

"I'm sorry," he said. "I didn't mean to wreck your day."

She shook her head and started walking a little faster, already planning on what she was going to say to Sierra when she saw her. She didn't want to come out of the gate accusing her. She needed to handle this delicately.

"I'm glad you did. I'd rather know than not know, even if I don't like the answer, if that makes sense."

"Well, for what it's worth, I hope we're both wrong, and none of your friends had anything to do with this."

"Me too," she said with a sigh. "I haven't been able to stop dwelling on what happened to Mariah. I've been terrified that someone at Iron and Flame is going to make a similar mistake and one of our guests will end up in the hospital or worse. I just wish I knew what happened. Even if Sierra *did* knock the EpiPen out of the way on purpose, it doesn't explain how Mariah had an allergic reaction to sesame when she wasn't anywhere near any sesame seeds or oil."

"Are you sure that's the only allergy she had?" Jude asked. "If you hadn't seen her for years, it's possible she developed a new allergy, or she had a rare one she didn't share with you back when you were friends."

It warmed her heart that Jude was trying to make her feel better, and for a moment, it worked, until she remembered something Cynthia had said. "It's possible, but I don't think it's likely. Cynthia said Mariah mentioned the sesame allergy when she ordered her food. If she had another allergy that was just as severe, she would have mentioned it as well. Trust me, when people have life-threatening allergies, they don't take chances or make assumptions."

"Well, either way, I don't think you should let it affect how you feel at work. I know you well enough by now to know how much you care about your restaurant and your customers. I have no doubt you're already doing the best you can to keep people safe, and that's all anyone can ask for."

Surprisingly, that did help. "Thanks, Jude," she said, glancing over at him with a weak smile. "That means a lot. That's the only thing that's made me feel better since Mariah's death. I'm already as careful as I can be, and unless I get superpowers, there isn't much more I can do."

"I'm glad it helped," he said, smiling back at her. "If you're still upset, I'm sure Saffron would be happy to give you more kisses."

That surprised a laugh out of her. "Thanks, but I don't think I'm quite that desperate yet."

FIVE

Lydia sent Sierra a text message to ask if she had time to get together today, then did her best to put the matter out of her mind for the rest of the hike. Despite the chill, it was a nice day, and something about being out in the woods was good for her soul.

By the time they got back to the parking lot, she was hungry enough to wish she had brought a snack. Sometimes, she and Jude went out to lunch together after their hike, but before she brought it up today, she checked her phone to see if Sierra had replied, and sure enough, a text message was waiting for her.

I'm free this afternoon if you want to come over. I just put a lasagna in the oven. It should be done in about an hour and a half, if you want lunch!

The text message seemed perfectly normal, not like her friend was struggling with remorse. Maybe her conversation with Jude had made her worry over nothing. Hopefully, seeing Sierra today would convince her they were on the wrong track.

"I had a really nice time," she told Jude as they stood by their vehicles. Saffron was already in his truck, her wet nose pressed against the window as she watched them. "Maybe we can get together for lunch sometime this week."

"I'd like that," he said. "Let me know if you need to talk about what happened to Mariah. I'm always happy to lend an ear."

"Thanks. I'm going to talk to Sierra next. I really hope she didn't have anything to do with the EpiPen disappearing."

"We're probably both overthinking it," he assured her.

She hoped he was right. Getting into her SUV, she started the engine and let it warm up while she responded to Sierra's text.

Sorry for not responding to this sooner. I was on a hike with Jude. I can be there in about 10 minutes, if that's not too soon.

She warmed her hands over the heat vents as she waited for a reply. It wasn't long before her phone chimed with a message telling her to come on over.

While she drove, she went over the conversation she wanted to have in her mind. She didn't want to sound accusatory. All that would achieve would be to put her friend on the defensive. She was sure that if Sierra *did* kick the EpiPen under the table, it had been a split-second decision. A horrible one, and one she probably regretted. If she was wrong, though, asking wouldn't achieve anything but to hurt her friend. It was going to be a delicate conversation either way.

Sierra lived in a subdivision on the outskirts of town. It was one of the newer communities in the area, and a sign of Quarry Creek's slowly growing economy. It used to be a mining town, and after the industry collapsed, it had faced some tough times. Now, with the resurgence of interest in hiking, camping, and other outdoor activities, and Quarry Creek's near-perfect location just north of Wausau near the Wisconsin River, it was seeing a surge of tourism.

The new industry brought in new jobs and new sources of income for the residents. Sierra worked as a trip planner and planned both local trips and trips abroad for customers all over the country. It was a lucrative job, judging by the size of the house she managed to afford on one income. Lydia knew Sierra had dated a handful of men since the fiasco with her fiancé, but she had yet to settle down. After such a major betrayal from not one but *two* people she had trusted, she wasn't surprised her friend had issues trusting again.

She parked in the driveway and shut her car off before grabbing her phone and her purse and walking up to the front door. In the silence after her knock, she heard a faint, "Come in!" from inside.

Letting herself through the unlocked door, she stepped into a spacious entry hall. There was a mat by the door for shoes, so she slipped hers off before walking down the hall towards the kitchen.

"Knock knock," she said as she peered through the doorway into the kitchen.

It was a spacious room, with quartz countertops, an island with a small bar and three stools, and a big window looking out into the backyard. The delicious, comforting scent of lasagna filled the air, and Lydia's stomach rumbled. All that hiking had made her hungry.

"Come on in and sit down," Sierra said. "I got your message just as I was taking the lasagna out of the oven. I got plates out for both of us. You do want to eat, right?"

"I can get something on my way home if you had other plans for the lasagna," Lydia said as she took a seat on one of the stools by the island.

Sarah laughed, shaking her head. "I'm going to set aside a few servings of this for later in the week, but I'm more than happy to share with you for lunch. I can't even count the number of times you've fed us, Miss Professional Chef. It's my turn. I'm going to let it cool for a second first, though. What do you want to drink? I have seltzer waters, juice, and some wine."

"A seltzer water is fine," Lydia said. "Thanks, Sierra. I'm sorry for springing this visit on you."

"Oh, I was happy to hear from you. I've barely seen you for the past couple of years. I know you've been busy with work, and I know how hard the divorce was for you, but I'm glad you're getting out there again. So, who is this Jude person you mentioned?"

"Oh, I didn't tell you about him?" Lydia said as she accepted the drink. "I met him a couple months ago. He tracked me down to warn me that one of his ex-coworkers was stalking me…"

She told Sierra all about her friendship with Jude while the other woman cut the lasagna, and they took turns chatting about their lives while they ate. The lasagna was delicious, with the perfect balance of cheese, meat, and sauce. Still, despite her hunger, it sat heavily in her stomach. Try as she might, she couldn't think of a good way to bring up what she wanted to ask.

Finally, she decided to just do it, and she broached the topic as gently as she could. "So, I keep thinking about what happened to Mariah at Morning Dove. It feels so unreal, you know? She shouldn't have died."

Sierra set her fork down. Her expression was uncertain. "Maybe it's karma. If anyone deserved what happened, it was her."

"Maybe," Lydia admitted. "But while I was talking to Jude today, I realized that one of us must have accidentally kicked her EpiPen under the table. Nothing else in her purse rolled so far when it spilled. I know I didn't, because I was standing too far away. Do you remember if your foot hit anything when the purse spilled?"

She made sure she wasn't outright accusing Sierra of anything. It didn't help, judging from the dark expression on her friend's face.

"Are you accusing me of kicking the EpiPen away?"

"I'm just trying to figure out what happened," Lydia said. "*One* of us had to have done it."

"And what, you think I'm the most likely suspect?"

A denial was on the tip of Lydia's tongue, but she held it back, because it was the truth. Out of all of them, Sierra had the most reason to hate Mariah. Her friend took her silence as the confirmation it was. She scoffed.

"I admit I hated Mariah. I will never forgive her for what she did, not in a hundred years, not whether she's alive or dead or even if she comes back as a ghost to apologize. But you're essentially accusing me of *murdering* her. It's been years. Why would I do it now? It's not like I'm the only person she's ever hurt. You *do* know why Taylor and Martin are getting a divorce, don't you?"

"I don't, actually," Lydia said. "We never got a chance to talk about it at the cafe."

"She found out Martin was cheating on her with Mariah," Sierra said, her tone clipped. "I called her later to get the full story, since she's my friend and I care about what she's going through. I can guarantee you Taylor hates Mariah just as much as I do, but with *her*, it's all still fresh."

"I had no idea about Martin," Lydia said.

"Obviously," Sierra snapped. She stood up, scraping her stool back across the floor. "And here I thought you were actually making an effort to reach out and be friends with us again. You only wanted to see me so you could ask if I hid Mariah's EpiPen, didn't you? That's rich, Lydia. I thought we could pick up where we left off and have our group back together again, but sometime over the past few years, you've changed a bit too much if you really think I would do something like that."

Sierra took Lydia's plate from in front of her and scraped the rest of her lasagna into the trash, then put the dish in the sink with a clatter. It was a clear dismissal, so Lydia, her face flaming, muttered a brief goodbye and hurried out of the house.

SIX

Lydia carefully hung the potted pothos back up above her kitchen sink. A few drops of water dripped out of the holes in the bottom and splattered against the stainless steel of the sink, leaving tiny specks of dirt behind after they rolled away. Lydia stared at them, feeling numb. What had started out as a lovely day now felt like a disaster.

She had a terrible feeling that she had wrecked her friendship with Sierra, a friendship that was just beginning to heal. And Sierra wasn't the only one she had hurt. Taylor's news about her divorce was huge, and Lydia hadn't called once over the past few days to check in with her. She had been so preoccupied with Mariah's death and her own concerns over the allergen policies at Iron and Flame that it hadn't even occurred to her to call her friend.

She was too self-absorbed, wasn't she? She had hurt one friend and neglected the other, when they had been kind enough to welcome her back into their group after she practically ghosted them for years.

With a deep sigh, she grabbed the dishrag from its spot hanging on the oven, mopped up the dirty drops of water from the pothos, then walked down the hall to the laundry room and tossed it into the washer. The rest of the weekend was no longer looking quite as bright as it had this morning.

She wanted to apologize to Sierra, but she thought it would be best to let the other woman cool off a little first. To make a bad matter worse, she still wasn't certain Sierra *hadn't* kicked the EpiPen out of the way, and now she had to wonder about Taylor as well. Or maybe neither of them did it. Maybe the device had hit the ground at the wrong angle and some strange accident of physics had sent it spinning off under the table on its own.

Or maybe one of them had kicked it by accident and hadn't even noticed. Could she really wreck her friendships over something that was nothing more than a half-baked theory between herself and Jude? But if she ignored it, would she ever be able to stop wondering if one of her friends had a hand in Mariah's death?

She didn't even feel like doing her usual weekend meal prepping, but she knew she would regret it if she didn't get started. She wanted to make something simple, so she put some potatoes on to boil and got out the rest of the ingredients for a creamy loaded potato soup. It would freeze well, and there wasn't much she would have to do other than boil the potatoes, fry the bacon, and then mix everything else together and give it a good jab with her immersion blender.

She was breaking one of the core tenets of cooking by staring at the pot of water, waiting for it to boil, when her phone buzzed. Hopeful that it was Sierra texting to apologize for lashing out, she looked away from the water to check the screen. The message was from Valerie, not Sierra, and seemed urgent judging by the number of exclamation marks after the words *Call me!!!*

Worried, she opened her friend's contact card and hit the button to call her. Her friend answered right away.

"Oh, thank goodness," Valerie said. "I just read something, and I need your expertise to tell me how grossed out and horrified I should be."

Maybe she had *one* friend left she hadn't completely alienated. Two, if she counted Jude, which she did. "I'm all ears."

"All right, so I was a bit curious about Mariah—you all seemed to know her and obviously I didn't—so I looked her up. Did you know she had a blog?"

"I had no idea. What did she write about?"

"A little bit of everything, it seems like. Whatever was going on in her life, reviews of recipes and restaurants... It was all pretty boring, if I'm being honest, but one post stood out to me. She wrote... I hesitate to even call it a review because it's just a lot of criticism, but it's about Morning Dove. She published it a week ago—just a few days before she died."

"She wrote a bad review about Morning Dove?" Lydia said.

The thought baffled her. Morning Dove was one of the most well-known places to eat in town. It tied with Iron and Flame for the most popular restaurant in the area, and the only reason they weren't direct competitors was because their hours barely intersected, and their menus were very different.

"Can I read it to you?"

"Go ahead."

Valerie cleared her throat. *"Just like everyone else in Quarry Creek, I used to love Morning Dove. It was the perfect place to stop in the morning for a quick, healthy breakfast and a delicious cup of coffee. The coffee was always hot, and the food was always cooked to perfection, and the service was always great. Or so I thought. When they hired my niece, I was ever so thrilled. But that's when things started going downhill. According to my niece, conditions in the kitchen were terrible. Dirty dishes, unswept floors, garbage that wasn't taken out for weeks. She swears she even saw rat droppings in the drawers. She quit on the spot when Cynthia refused to improve the conditions. I am disgusted with the restaurant's behavior, but I'm so proud of my niece for standing up for herself and coming out with the truth. Let this be a warning to all of you. Do not eat at Morning Dove until we see evidence that things have changed. Miss Mariah, signing off."*

"She wrote that?" Lydia said, shocked.

"I know, right? Do you think she's telling the truth? I eat there all the time. I'm starting to feel sick just thinking about it."

"Cynthia gave me a tour of her kitchen once, but it was a few years ago. When I saw it, everything was clean and tidy. Things could have changed, but it doesn't sound like the Cynthia I know."

"Either way, this is big, isn't it?" Valerie said. "I mean, maybe Cynthia saw this and wanted to get revenge on Mariah. Maybe what happened wasn't an accident after all."

Lydia felt a chill that had nothing to do with the winter weather outside. This entire time, she had been assuming that however Mariah came into contact with an allergen, it had been an accident. A freak occurrence, where maybe Cynthia was technically, *legally* at fault, but had never actually intended to hurt anyone. But with the blog post Valerie had found, she had to wonder if there was something else going on. Maybe it wasn't an accident at all.

Maybe there was something more insidious than a misplaced EpiPen to worry about.

But then she remembered how frantic Cynthia had been in the bathroom when she was trying to get Mariah to keep breathing.

"I don't know," she said slowly. "Cynthia seemed like she was really upset, and I don't think she was faking it."

"She could have been having second thoughts," Valerie suggested. "Maybe she didn't realize how severe the allergic reaction would be."

"Even if she thought Mariah would just get some hives and have to go to the hospital, something like that could wreck her reputation, especially combined with the review on Mariah's blog. Cynthia's never been more than an acquaintance, so I don't know her extremely well, but I do know she loves Morning Dove. I don't think she would jeopardize it on purpose."

"I guess, but you have to admit, it seems kind of suspicious," Valerie said. "It does, doesn't it? I'm not crazy?"

"It does," Lydia admitted with a sigh. "I just can't see why she would risk it."

"Well, maybe we're missing something. Do you think I should tell someone else? Do you think the police know?"

"I'm sure they found out about Mariah's blog by now, but it can't hurt to forward the blog post to them," Lydia said. "I do understand where you're coming from, Valerie. I'm not saying you're wrong. I just…"

She trailed off, unable to explain to her friend why she was so reluctant to jump to conclusions. It had turned out terribly the last time she did it.

"Well, I'll send it to the police," Valerie said. "At least you don't think I've gone completely off the wall. I don't think I'm going to be eating at Morning Dove for a while, though."

As much as Lydia hated to admit it, a meal at the café sounded less appealing than ever to her as well. She did want to talk to Cynthia, though. Maybe once it reopened, she could stop in and ask Cynthia if she could take another look at her kitchen. She wasn't sure what she was hoping to find. If the kitchen was clean and tidy like it should be, then it would mean

Mariah's blog post was a lie, which in turn meant that Cynthia might have a stronger motive to hurt her.

If the kitchen was as disgusting as the blog post said, Lydia doubted she would ever be able to eat at the cafe again. Unsanitary kitchens were nightmare fuel to her.

SEVEN

Doubt was a terrible thing to live with. Lydia had grown up in Quarry Creek, and after culinary school, she had returned to make her life here. This town was very much her home. She thought she knew the people who lived here. But now, she was beginning to wonder if she was wrong. Sierra, Taylor, even Cynthia... She had known all of them for years. Was her uncertainty about whether one of them had something to do with Mariah's death a sign that she didn't know them as well as she thought she did, or was it a sign that something was wrong with *her*? Maybe she wasn't the person she thought she was, if she could suspect her friends of a horrible crime so easily.

After the weekend, she tried to get back to a semblance of normalcy, though she was more distracted in the kitchen than usual. She paused to see if Morning Dove was open whenever she passed the little café, but even well into the next week, it hadn't reopened. She was beginning to wonder if it ever would.

It was Thursday, a little over a week since Mariah's death, when Taylor finally responded to the text message Lydia had sent her over the weekend, asking how she was doing. It wasn't much, but after how terribly her conversation with Sierra had gone, she hadn't been in the right mental space to have a real sit-down conversation with Taylor.

Taylor's response was a polite, cheerful text message asking if she wanted to meet at Iron and Flame today for lunch. Lydia had the evening shift today, which meant she didn't have to be at the restaurant until four. She sent a text back, asking if Taylor wanted to meet at two. That would give them enough time to chat, and if their lunch didn't take as long as she expected, she could start her shift a little early. Jeremy could just deal with it if he didn't like sharing a kitchen with her for an hour.

Taylor beat her to the restaurant. She must have said something to Jaelin, the hostess on shift, about meeting Lydia, because as soon as Jaelin saw her enter the restaurant, she gestured toward the table Taylor was at. Lydia thanked her with a smile, then walked through the restaurant to join her friend.

"Thanks for meeting me," Taylor said. "Sorry it took me so long to text you back. I've been a little distracted, as you can probably imagine."

"Don't worry about it," Lydia said. "I was feeling bad for not reaching out sooner. What happened to Mariah hit me hard, I guess. I'm so worried about it happening to one of our guests."

Taylor's expression softened into one of understanding and sympathy. "Oh my gosh, I didn't even make that connection. I'm sure you don't have anything to worry about, Lydia. You're such a good chef, and you've got great employees. Who knows what happened to Mariah, but I'm sure whatever it was, it won't happen here."

"Thanks. I'm sorry for not being there for you if you needed me, though. I know what you're going through, and I know how important support is. I never even put you in contact with my lawyer."

"Just text me her information when you get a chance," Taylor said. "I hate to bring it up, but what on earth happened with you and Sierra? I spoke with her on Sunday, and she was *mad* at you. Did you really accuse her of kicking the EpiPen under the table on purpose?"

"Not exactly. The conversation just got out of hand," Lydia said with a groan. "I just thought ... well, you know how much she hated Mariah."

"I know she already told you, but I want to bring it up just in case. Martin was having an affair with Mariah, which is why we're getting a divorce. After Sierra told me what you said to her, and now that you know I have a very good reason to hate that witch too, I have to ask... Do you think *I* had something to do with her death?"

Lydia hesitated. She didn't know what to say. "Honestly, Taylor, it was probably just an accident. Everything was chaos, and any of us could have easily kicked the EpiPen under the table without noticing."

"You're always going to wonder if one of us did it on purpose, though, aren't you?" Taylor asked.

"Well, wouldn't you?" Lydia said. "Just think about it from my perspective. I *know* how much Sierra—and now you—hated Mariah. I don't blame you for feeling that way. She was a monster. All it would take would be a split second where you wanted to hurt her as much as she hurt you."

"Do you really think so little of us?" Taylor asked. "Can't you just realize that we're your friends and you know us? You should know neither of us would do something like that."

"I'm just trying to figure out what happened, that's all." Hoping she could smooth things over, she added, "I recently found out that a few days before she died, Mariah wrote a bad review of Morning Dove on her blog. I've known Cynthia for years, but now I'm second-guessing everything. The blog post accused her of having a disgusting kitchen, and even though I've seen her kitchen with my own two eyes, I can't stop wondering if she really let it get that bad. I can't stop wondering if she wanted to get revenge for that bad review and slipped a few sesame seeds into the coffee grinder when she saw Mariah come in that morning. I just ... something about what happened to Mariah really bothers me. It never should have happened in the first place, and when it did, her EpiPen should have been right there, with everything else that was in her purse. Too many coincidences led to her death."

"You're really not going to drop it?" Taylor asked, her voice sharp with annoyance. "You hurt Sierra, and I'm starting to feel kind of hurt too. You should trust us because we're your *friends*. As to whether Cynthia did something, who knows? You're a chef, not a cop. It's not your job to figure this out. You didn't *see* anyone kick the EpiPen out of the way, did you? You didn't *see* anyone slip a sesame seed into Mariah's coffee?"

"You know I didn't."

"So just *let it go*. Let the police do their jobs and focus on patching things up with Sierra. I respect you a lot, Lydia, but sometimes I think you take everything too seriously."

"A woman *died*. If I'm not supposed to take that seriously, then what?"

Taylor sighed. "I know you're coming from a place of good intentions. But we all witnessed the same thing you did, and the rest of us? We drew together. Sierra and I have spent hours talking since last week. Even

Valerie called, and we chatted for a while, and I barely know the woman. There were no accusations, no hard feelings, nothing negative. Now here you are, throwing around all sorts of wild theories. You're making it really hard to be your friend right now, Lydia."

That stung.

"Well, if that's how you feel, I'm sorry. I don't think I accused anyone of anything. I'm just trying to figure out what happened. I shouldn't have to apologize for how much Mariah's death is bothering me."

"You don't have to." Taylor stood up and grabbed her coat from the back of her chair. "But you *do* have to apologize for hurting your friends. We'll be here when you're ready, but until you drop this ... this weird obsession with crime solving, I think we need to take a break from each other."

With that, she turned and walked away, leaving Lydia sitting alone at the table.

EIGHT

The sight of Morning Dove's open sign glowing with welcoming neon letters the next morning filled Lydia with a feeling of resignation. It seemed like everything she had done so far was wrong, but she still wanted to talk to Cynthia. Questions about Mariah aside, she felt a professional responsibility to make sure Cynthia's kitchen wasn't unsafe. She was no health inspector, but she couldn't bear the thought of someone eating food that came out of a kitchen with the conditions described in Mariah's blog post.

She had the morning shift today, and Iron and Flame didn't open until eleven. It was a little before ten, so she had the time to stop by the café as long as she was quick. It took a while to open properly and start preparing some of the more time-consuming dishes, but the cafe would be closed by the time she left the restaurant later that day, so this was her only chance to talk to Cynthia unless she wanted to wait until tomorrow.

The café wasn't very busy. Only two tables were occupied, and one of those tables was filled with a group of teenagers who were whispering to each other and looking around like the cafe was the most fascinating thing they had ever seen. Two of them had their phones out and looked like they were taking pictures of the surrounding booths and the floor. She wondered if they were drawn to the morbidity of eating at a restaurant where someone had died. The thought of Cynthia having to deal with all of the negative publicity made her feel bad, but she knew there wasn't much she could do about it. Small towns loved gossip, and a sudden, mysterious death was just about the juiciest gossip they could get.

"I'll be right with you; sit anywhere you like!" Cynthia called from the kitchen in response to the bell that jingled above the door when Lydia walked in.

Lydia was in a bit of a hurry, but not enough to rush Cynthia when she was obviously busy, so she took a seat at a table near the register and waited. Before too long, Cynthia came out of the kitchen with a tray that was absolutely loaded down with food. She nodded at Lydia in greeting as she passed by on her way to the table full of teenagers. After passing out their plates, she came up to Lydia's table, the tray tucked under her arm. She had circles under her eyes, and looked like she hadn't slept in a week.

"Hey. What can I get for you?"

"I was hoping you had time to talk, but it looks like I might need to come back."

Cynthia shook her head, giving a weak laugh. "It's not a great time, but when is these days? If you want to talk, come on back into the kitchen with me. I need to keep working."

Since part of the reason Lydia was there was to see the kitchen, she wasn't about to argue with that. She rose to her feet and followed Cynthia through the swinging door behind the counter. The instant she stepped into the kitchen, she knew Mariah's blog post had been full of lies. Either that, or Cynthia had used all the time the cafe was closed to do a deep cleaning. It was as spick-and-span as Lydia's own kitchen was. Not a single thing raised a red flag, and she would have been comfortable cooking a meal in here herself.

She didn't realize that she had paused and was scrutinizing the kitchen until Cynthia sighed. "You read that terrible blog post, didn't you?"

"Yeah," Lydia said, wincing. "Sorry, a friend of mine pointed it out to me over the weekend, and I haven't been able to get it out of my mind."

"That's fine, at least you actually came here to check things out for yourself instead of assuming it was true. The whole thing was lies. Well, not the part about Mariah's niece working here. That was true, though I wish it wasn't."

"Why? And why would she make all of that up?"

Cynthia started washing her hands, talking as she scrubbed them. "Well, I hired Ava about a month ago. At first, things were fine. She was an average employee. A little distractible, but nothing too bad. I had some issues with her being on her phone too much from the very beginning, but I didn't realize how much of an issue it was until I caught her making a video of the kitchen floor. Obviously, I was confused about what she was doing. She had scattered raisins all over the floor, and when I made her show me the video, it was a recording of her telling people they were rat feces. She had an account on one of those video sharing websites, and I guess the videos she was posting of her faking gross restaurant conditions were getting a lot of traffic, so she kept getting more and more extreme."

"Yikes," Lydia said. "I would have been livid."

"Oh, I was. I fired her on the spot. There's no excuse for doing that. I know she was young—she had just turned sixteen when I hired her—and she might not have realized how damaging those videos could be to the restaurant, but I couldn't overlook the lack of judgment."

"I wouldn't be able to either."

"A couple days later, Mariah released that blog post," Cynthia said with a sigh as she started slicing potatoes. "I'm sure Ava went crying to her aunt with all sorts of lies about why I fired her, but thankfully, I made her delete those videos from her account before I let her go, so she didn't even have any fake 'proof' to back up her aunt's post. A few people have come in to ask me about it, but I'm always happy to show them the kitchen if they want to see it, which seems to help their worries."

"Thanks for explaining everything. I knew it sounded off, but knowing what really happened helps."

"I don't blame you," Cynthia said. "No one likes a gross kitchen, especially not people who work in the restaurant industry. Last week's tragedy couldn't have happened at a worse time. The police learned about the blog post, of course. It didn't look good considering what happened to Mariah just a few days after she published it."

"Is that why it took you so long to reopen?"

She nodded. "They spent a lot of time questioning me, and they got a health inspector out to go through my kitchen with a fine-tooth comb. They gave me the all clear to open a couple days ago, completely out of the blue. I don't know if they found a new lead, or if they realized that they weren't going to find anything incriminating in my kitchen no matter how hard they looked. I mean, sure, I have buns with sesame seeds on them and some sesame oil that I haven't used since that Thai chicken salad special I offered over the summer, but she didn't have anything but coffee while she was here."

"They didn't tell you why you were no longer a suspect?"

"Nope, but I'm not going to look a gift horse in the mouth. I wish I knew what happened to her, though. I swear, there's no way any sort of sesame *anything* could have contaminated her coffee, but until I'm certain about what happened, I'm always going to wonder if it was something I did."

"I understand," Lydia said. "It's been bothering me too. I've been ridiculously careful about every allergy request we get at the restaurant. And we already have very strict allergy policies. I think I'm driving my employees crazy, but I'm terrified I'm going to miss something."

"Well, if I find out what happened, I'll let you know," Cynthia said. "Even if it was a mistake I made, somehow. If I can stop it from happening to anyone else, I want to."

Lydia felt like she and Cynthia understood each other. What happened to Mariah was any chef's worse nightmare. No matter what the cause was, as soon as Lydia knew what happened, her own policies were going to change to make sure it could never happen at Iron and Flame.

NINE

Talking to Cynthia made her feel a little better, both because Cynthia understood her concerns, and because the confirmation of a clean kitchen meant she wouldn't have to stop eating at her favorite restaurant ... well, her favorite that wasn't Iron and Flame.

On the other hand, the conversation had left her more puzzled than ever. She thought Cynthia was being honest when she said she had no idea why Mariah had an allergic reaction, but all that meant was that they were missing something important.

When she got to Iron and Flame, she started her normal opening routine, and once the kitchen was ready for the day, she decided to walk through what happened in Cynthia's kitchen the day of Mariah's death. She started the coffee maker, grabbed a mug and saucer, rolled some silverware up into a napkin, then put her hands on her hips. Coffee, mug, saucer, silverware, napkin. Other than the booth and the table, those were the only things Mariah had touched.

Cynthia had mentioned she had sesame seed buns and sesame oil, the latter of which she hadn't used since the summer. Working under the assumption that the woman was telling the truth, that meant the sesame seed buns were the most likely culprit.

She could understand if a sesame seed had fallen off a bun and had gotten stuck somewhere strange. A single sesame seed left behind on a booth was far from impossible, but that seed then had to get into something Mariah had consumed.

And the only thing she had consumed was coffee. The mugs at Morning Dove were stored upside down on the tables, so a sesame seed falling into a mug at some point before Cynthia poured Mariah's coffee didn't make any sense. Maybe it had been stuck to the rim, but that seemed like a stretch.

Mariah probably would have noticed it when she took a sip or when she stirred her coffee.

Maybe it had been stuck to the spoon she stirred her coffee with. Taking the spoon out of the rolled-up napkin, Lydia considered it. If Cynthia washed the spoon with a plate that had a few sesame seeds leftover from a burger bun on it, maybe the seed had gotten stuck to the surface of the spoon during the dishwasher cycle, then came off when Mariah stirred her coffee.

The swinging door to the kitchen opened. Chartreuse, one of their sous chefs, walked in with a cheerful, "Hey, how are you doing?" She paused part way across the kitchen to add, "*What* are you doing?"

Lydia realized she probably looked ridiculous, squinting at a spoon while standing in front of an empty coffee mug with one hand on her hip. She put the spoon down and heaved a heavy sigh.

"My version of a crime scene reenactment, I guess."

"Ah, what happened at Morning Dove is still bothering you?" the younger woman asked as she hung her coat up in the nook reserved for the employees' items and went over to the sink to wash her hands.

All of her employees knew the story of Mariah's death by now. She had even gotten Jeremy on board with reviewing their policies surrounding allergies. It had shaken her to the core, because it was something that could easily happen in her own restaurant if they were careless even once.

"I talked with Cynthia earlier," she admitted as she poured herself a cup of coffee—she needed the energy; she hadn't been sleeping well lately. "We talked about what happened, and from what she says, it should have been next to impossible for sesame seeds or oil to have contaminated the coffee. She hasn't even used her sesame oil in months. I was thinking a sesame seed might have gotten stuck to the silverware or the coffee mug Mariah was using. I know how unlikely it sounds, but it's the only possibility I can think of."

"Would a single sesame seed really be enough for that sort of reaction?" Chartreuse asked. "I know some people are very sensitive to whatever they're allergic to, but if she was *that* sensitive, she probably wouldn't take the risk of eating out. I have a cousin who is extremely allergic to peanuts, to the point where he gets a reaction if he's even in the same room as peanuts or that powdered peanut butter stuff, but he's very careful when he's out in public and never eats out anywhere, because he knows how easy cross-contamination would be even at a careful restaurant."

"I have no idea, but what else could it be? If you have any ideas, I'd love to hear them."

"Personally, I think she had another allergy no one knew about," Chartreuse said. "You said she drank some coffee, right? Maybe she had a reaction to an artificial sweetener or one of those non-dairy cream products. I know stuff like oat milk and almond milk has been getting more popular; maybe she poured some into her coffee without noticing."

"If she knew she was allergic to something else, why wouldn't she have double checked what she was putting into her coffee? I used to be friends with her, and she was always very careful about checking ingredients for anything sesame related. I can't imagine she got *less* careful over the years."

"I don't know," Chartreuse admitted. "It could have been something she wasn't aware she was allergic to, I guess. Some really obscure preservative or something she hadn't come across before."

Lydia frowned. She had been going to Morning Dove regularly for years, and as far as she remembered, Cynthia always had the same brands of creamer and the same types of sugar and sweetener packets on the tables. Even the coffee always tasted the same—she wasn't sure if Cynthia ground it herself or not, but she was pretty sure she bought it from a bulk restaurant supply store. It was nothing fancy, and she doubted the other woman had switched brands out of the blue. People were picky about their coffee, and her customers would complain if she changed it unexpectedly.

With a jolt, she remembered Valerie complaining about how her coffee tasted. Lydia had tasted her coffee as well, and it tasted normal to her, but Valerie had put creamer into hers. Dairy creamer, the stuff that was supposed to be refrigerated. She had completely forgotten that Taylor had switched it for the dish of creamers at Mariah's table, but her conversation with Chartreuse had brought it back to her.

Was the bad creamer connected to Mariah's reaction? As far as she knew, spoiled milk wasn't any more likely to cause an allergic reaction than regular milk, and she didn't remember Mariah having any problems with dairy.

Now that she thought of it, she couldn't let the thought go. In the past, Cynthia had always brought out a little saucer of chilled milk or cream if someone asked for it, and she had never had those little plastic containers of real dairy creamer. The creamer in the bowls on the tables was always the fake stuff that didn't need to be refrigerated. So where had the little containers of real dairy creamer come from?

The answer seemed obvious when she thought about it. Ava, Mariah's niece. According to Cynthia, she had been making fake videos about the "disgusting" conditions at Morning Dove to get more views online. Leaving some dairy creamers out to go bad and then catching the customer's reaction on video seemed like it might fit with what she was doing, but she had gotten fired before she could complete her plan.

That might explain where the little dish of spoiled dairy creamers had come from, but it still didn't explain what happened to Mariah ... unless Ava had done something else to the creamers. Maybe she had contaminated them somehow, maybe even unintentionally. And since she had been fired before Mariah died, the police might not have questioned her.

"Do you want me to get started on the roast?"

Lydia blinked, forcing her attention back to the real world. Theories and educated guesses would have to wait. Right now, she had to focus on her job.

"Yeah, go ahead. I'm going to start a new batch of chicken stock. I noticed we're running low."

She needed to be mentally present in the kitchen right now, but later this evening, she intended to try to track down Ava and see if the younger woman would be willing to talk to her. Even if it was a prank gone wrong, Cynthia and everyone else connected to Mariah and her death deserved answers about what happened.

TEN

Tracking down Ava turned out to be a lot harder than she expected. When she searched for Ava's name on the social media app on her phone, a lot of results popped up, but none of the Avas shared Mariah's last name. Which shouldn't have been surprising since, if she was remembering correctly, Mariah had two sisters and no brothers, which meant her niece would share a last name with whoever her mother had married.

But Lydia had been friends with Mariah for years. For the life of her, she couldn't remember even the first names of either of Mariah's sisters, and when she tried to find Mariah's social media page, she found that it had already been set to private. She wouldn't be able to look at her friends page to track down her family members. Which was probably a good thing, because when she thought about it like that, it sounded a little creepy.

She felt like she was onto something with the spoiled creamers, though. They were the one thing that stood out about that day—well, other than Mariah's death, of course. The creamers were so out of place that they had to mean *something*, and if her intuition was right, then Ava was the one who had planted them in the restaurant. She wanted to know if she had done anything else to them.

She thought about calling Cynthia to ask for Ava's number or even just her full name, but that was a little too far for her. She would have to explain why she wanted to talk to Ava, which meant revealing that she was looking into Mariah's death, and she wasn't sure how the other woman would take it. She also suspected Cynthia would be hesitant to give her the contact information for an ex-employee. The more she thought about it, the more she became convinced it was a bad idea. She certainly wouldn't give any of *her* employees' contact information out, regardless of whether they were a past or present employee, or if they had left on bad terms.

It was possible Taylor or Sierra would know Ava's full name. It was a long shot, but she needed to talk to her friends anyway. After yesterday's conversation with Taylor, she knew she had to make amends. She decided to kill two birds with one stone and call Taylor to see if they could set up another lunch for this coming weekend—her treat. Talking to Ava was the only idea she had left when it came to solving the mystery of Mariah's death, so if Taylor asked her, she could honestly swear that she was going to drop her amateur investigation after this.

She dialed her friend's number, a little worried that she would get sent straight to voicemail, and was relieved when Taylor picked up after just a few rings. Maybe she was forgiven after all.

"Hello, Taylor Oliver speaking."

Or maybe not. It sounded like her friend had answered the phone without checking the caller ID first.

"Hey, Taylor. It's Lydia. Do you have time to talk?"

There was a muffled noise, and when Taylor spoke again, her voice was much clearer; Lydia realized she must have been on speakerphone before.

"I don't know, do *you* have time to talk?" Taylor asked, her tone snippy. "Because judging from the radio silence before you called, the answer is no."

"I saw you just yesterday," Lydia said. "I haven't been ignoring you. I had to work after you walked out on our lunch, and I had another shift this morning."

"You didn't even have five minutes to spare to send me that lawyer information you keep promising to give me?"

"Considering the way our conversation ended, it didn't sound like you wanted to talk to me at all. I'll send the information as soon as we get off the phone." She felt her temper heating up and took a deep breath, trying to calm herself down. "Look, Taylor, I'm sorry. If you need more time to cool off, that's fine. But I don't think it's fair for you to get mad at me when it's only been a day since we last spoke, and the last words you said to me were that you thought we needed to take a break from each other. I was just giving you space—which I thought you wanted."

She heard her friend sigh. "You're right, that wasn't fair of me. I know it's not an excuse, but I've been all over the place emotionally. I've been a complete mess since I found out about Martin. I know I was a jerk yesterday, and honestly, I felt bad as soon as I left. So, I'll apologize for that, but this isn't all my fault. I needed your support this week, and you never once offered it."

"I know. I'm sorry. What happened to Mariah—"

"No," Taylor bit out, her tone sharpening. "You don't get to use that as an excuse. I know Mariah's death shook you up, and I get that, but I'm going through a divorce. I thought that you, of all people, would know what I'm going through. Sierra and I were both there for you when you went through your divorce, but you can't even take the time to text me a phone number or give me a call to see how I'm doing? Can you see why I'm so mad? What's happening to me, your *friend*, should be more important to you than what happened to Mariah—who is the reason my marriage is falling apart in the first place. She deserved what happened to her. I don't deserve what's happening to me. I don't deserve to be going through this alone!"

With that, the line went dead. Lydia stared at her cell phone, wondering how everything had gone so terribly wrong so quickly.

Was Taylor right? Was she being a terrible friend? Maybe there was something wrong with her, because no matter how she looked at it, and no matter how bad she felt for Taylor, she just couldn't see a divorce as being more important than a woman's *death*. A death she had witnessed personally. It didn't lessen what Taylor was going through, but she didn't think she was wrong for having Mariah's death on her mind so much.

Either way, Taylor was hurt. And if she didn't do anything to help, then she really would be a terrible friend.

Her search for Ava was going to have to wait. She opened her contacts app and found Sierra's number, dialing it before she could second-guess herself. Sierra was probably still mad at her too, but hopefully she would be able to set her feelings aside for the time being and help Lydia patch things up with Taylor. When she was sitting alone in her house after she and Jeremy finalized their divorce papers, her friends had come over laden down with junk food, chocolate, and wine to keep her company. It was high time they did something like that for Taylor now that she was going through the same thing Lydia had.

ELEVEN

Convincing Sierra to help her surprise Taylor was easier than she expected, probably because she volunteered to do all the hard work. She called a takeout order in to Iron and Flame, and being intimately familiar with how long all of the food took to prepare, knew she had just enough time to swing by the grocery store before she picked it up. She grabbed two bottles of wine, a sumptuous looking chocolate cake from the bakery section, and a box of microwave popcorn.

After picking up the food from Iron and Flame, she texted Sierra to let her know she was on her way over to Taylor's house, and drove the once familiar route to the cozy brick house Taylor and Martin had lived in together for the majority of their marriage. The thought made a lump form in her throat. She really hadn't been a great friend to Taylor. She didn't think she was wrong for caring about what happened to Mariah, but she should have put in the extra effort to be there for Taylor too.

She parked along the curb in front of the house. Sierra had timed it well enough that she arrived just as Lydia was getting out of her SUV. Both of them were in comfortable clothes—there was no need to dress up, not for an evening like this—and Sierra was even in her sweatpants. It brought her back to a different time; not necessarily a better one, but a nostalgic one, when she was newly single and she and her friends spent almost every weekend together, chatting and gossiping and just enjoying girl time.

"Did you get everything?" Sierra asked as she peered at all of the bags in the passenger seat footwell.

"I did. Can you grab the bags from the grocery store?"

Sierra nodded, hefting the bags of groceries while Lydia took the takeout bags from Iron and Flame. After bumping her car door shut with her hip, she followed Sierra up the walkway to Taylor's front door. With her hands full, Sierra knocked on the door with her boot, a heavy, thudding sound.

There were small windows on either side of the door, and Lydia saw the sheer curtains over one of them twitch as Taylor peered out at them. A flash of surprised gratitude crossed her face, and she opened the door.

"Lydia? Sierra? Did you really do all this for me, even though I've been such a ... well, I haven't been very fun to be around lately?"

"Maybe you could have phrased some of the things you said differently, but you were right," Lydia said as Taylor stepped out of the way to let them inside. "I should have been here for you more than I was. I know this can't make up for it completely, but hopefully it's a start. Thanks for knocking some sense into me."

"I still think Lydia has to work through some issues, but I'm prepared to forgive and forget for the sake of friendship," Sierra grumbled. "She got all the food, so that helps."

Taylor looked genuinely touched, and Lydia knew she had made the right decision. The three of them might have their differences and disagreements, but if they couldn't come together for something as important and life changing as Taylor's divorce, then could they even call themselves friends?

Taylor's house was a cozy three bedroom, one and a half bath, two-story brick house on one of the older and nicer residential streets in Quarry Creek. Two of the bedrooms were upstairs, and the third was a converted office downstairs. There was a small, formal dining room right off the kitchen, and a large living room that took up most of the rest of the first floor.

Lydia set the takeout bags from Iron and Flame down on the dining room table while Sierra took the other bags into the kitchen. She had ordered a few entrees for them to share. She knew the glazed honey salmon was a favorite of Taylor's, and the two steaks and order of pasta she had gotten in addition to the fish was more than enough to leave Taylor with leftovers even after all three of them ate.

She had gotten plenty of sides as well and set everything out nicely on the table while her friends brought in the dishes, silverware, and a pitcher of water. Taylor looked so touched that it made Lydia's heart ache to think of how much sooner she should have done this.

"I really am sorry," she said as they sat down and began serving themselves food. "I hope I can make it up to you."

"Well, you're here now," Taylor said. She gave Lydia a light, teasing smile that told her they were on good terms again. "But you never did get me your lawyer's number. I'm starting to think you've got a mental block around it."

"I'll do it right now," Lydia said. She searched through her phone for the right contact card and sent the information to Taylor.

After the other woman thanked her, Sierra said, "So, is it too early to plan a girls' night out at the bar and find you a hot date?"

Taylor shook her head, a smile still on her lips. "I think I'm going to hold off on dating for a while. I'm still in the swearing off men stage. I hope it doesn't take me as long as it took Lydia to get back into the dating game, though. What has it been, four years, and you're just starting to date now?"

"I'm not dating," Lydia said. "I'm just ... casually going on hikes with someone."

"Oh yeah, your game warden," Sierra said. "He's kind of like law enforcement, but for deer and stuff, right? Is he why you're so into mysteries now?"

"Not exactly, but he does work with the police sometimes, and he mentioned that they were investigating her death as a possible homicide, which I'll admit is what kicked all of this off." She had spoken without thinking, falling back into the habit of sharing everything with her friends, and realized she should have kept quiet about it like he had asked. "Maybe don't mention that. I don't think he was supposed to share it with me."

Taylor frowned. "Did he say why they thought it was a homicide? I mean, we were all there. We all saw that she didn't even talk to anyone but Cynthia."

"No, he didn't. I think both of you were right, and I need to let it go." She thought briefly about bringing up Ava and the question of where the dairy creamers had come from but decided against it. That would probably just start off another argument, and they weren't here for her. They were here for Taylor. If she decided to pursue it later, she could figure out another way to hunt down Ava's contact information. She decided to change the subject. "I don't know if you have plans later this evening, Taylor, but if not, I was thinking we could watch a movie, gorge ourselves on chocolate, and drink some wine. I brought popcorn, too."

"Oh, or we could start watching a TV show. I know one that the two of you would love."

"My life is sad right now, so no, I didn't have any plans," Taylor said. "A movie or TV show sounds great to me. And I could use some of that wine now, if you're offering. This salmon deserves to be paired with something better than water."

"I'll go get it, you don't have to get up," Lydia said. "The glasses are still in the same spot?"

Taylor nodded. "There's a corkscrew in the drawer by the sink. Martin took the good one, but I ordered another one online."

Lydia got up and walked into the kitchen. Taylor wasn't as much of a cook as she was, but she and

Martin were well-off and the kitchen was modern, with much nicer appliances than Lydia had in the kitchen of her rental house.

She saw the bottle of Malbec she had bought sitting on the kitchen counter, but the Riesling wasn't in sight. Wondering if one of the others had put it in the fridge, she pulled open the stainless-steel door and looked inside. From the sight of the containers on the fridge shelves, it was evident that Taylor had been living off of takeout recently, and she felt another pang of guilt. She really should have been there for her friend.

Sure enough, the Riesling was in the door of the fridge. She reached for the bottle of wine, but paused when she saw what it was sitting next to. A carton of something that, at first glance, looked like almond milk, but when she took in the words on the carton, her heart stopped.

Sesame milk. She picked up the carton, turning it over in her hands as she read the ingredients and description. *Unsweetened white sesame milk. Vegan, dairy free, soy and nut free, gluten-free. Ingredients; Water, sesame.*

And there, on a shelf right in front of her, at eye level, was a bowl full of little plastic containers of creamer that claimed they were real dairy. She thought of the bowl of identical creamers at the cafe, of Taylor's smirk when she carried them over to Mariah's table, of Mariah stirring creamer into her coffee before she started itching. Clutching the carton too tightly in one hand, she shut the fridge door and carried the carton of sesame milk into the dining room.

TWELVE

Taylor and Sierra were laughing as Lydia walked back into the dining room. Sierra looked up, her eyes narrowing slightly in concern.

"Couldn't you find the wine? I put it in the door of the fridge."

Taylor looked up too, a smile still on her face, but the expression froze when she spotted the carton of sesame milk in Lydia's hand.

"I found the wine," Lydia said faintly. Her pulse was pounding in her ears. Even with the evidence in her hands, a part of her mind was still trying to convince herself that she was wrong.

"Um, no you didn't," Sierra said, her face full of confusion. "That's milk, Lydia."

Somehow it seemed to take her forever to cross the room. Finally, she reached the table and set the carton down on it. "It's sesame milk."

Sierra just blinked. Taylor was still frozen, though the smile had faded from her face. Her words were stiff when she spoke. "Why did you bring that out here? I don't think it will go very well with the salmon."

"I saw the dairy creamers in your fridge too," Lydia said, holding her gaze.

"I drink a lot of coffee," Taylor replied.

"They were the same brand as the ones at Morning Dove. And Morning Dove has never had dairy creamers before."

"What's going on?" Sierra said.

Taylor didn't look at her. She didn't do anything for a long moment, until her lips wobbled. "Please don't do this, Lydia."

"What did you do?" Lydia whispered.

"What are you talking about?" Sierra asked. "I don't—" She fell silent, her eyes going wide as she looked at the sesame milk. Lydia could tell she was putting it together. Slowly, she turned to look at their other friend. "Taylor? Please tell me Lydia's going completely insane."

"Can we get back to our nice evening?" Taylor asked. Her voice was shaking. "Please? I don't want to talk about this."

"*How* did you do it?" Lydia asked. She was convinced this was a nightmare. It was impossible that one of her friends had killed someone. Impossible.

"Lydia... You don't really think she... I mean, we all hate Mariah, but she wouldn't..."

Sierra fell silent as Taylor slowly bowed her head, dragging her hands through her hair. "She stole my husband from me, Lydia. You would've done the same thing."

"No, I wouldn't have," Lydia said. It was the only thing she felt certain about right now. Jeremy had never had an affair, but even if he had, she didn't think anything would be able to drive her to kill another person in cold blood.

"*Taylor.* Tell me what's going on." Sierra crossed her arms. She looked both frightened and angry, as if she wasn't quite sure how to feel.

"Mariah was a terrible person," Taylor said. "Think of all the lives she wrecked. She went after men in committed relationships on purpose. I know for a fact that Sierra and I weren't the only ones whose lives she wrecked. It's not like she was innocent. No one is going to miss her."

"That's not the point," Lydia said. Inside her head, she felt like screaming and crying, but her voice was surprisingly even. It felt far too similar to how she had felt when she finally realized her and Jeremy's relationship was over. "You killed someone."

"I don't *understand*," Sierra snapped. "Stop ignoring me. How? Sure, there's sesame milk here, but how did she make Mariah drink it? We were both there, we both saw that she didn't even talk to Mariah."

"It was the creamers, wasn't it?" Lydia prodded when Taylor didn't answer. "You switched out the dairy inside for this sesame milk."

Finally, Taylor gave a tight nod of her head. "I thought it was the perfect crime. I spent ages figuring out how to open those little plastic containers without tearing the foil on top, and then even longer figuring out how to seal them back down so no one would notice. I changed out the dairy for sesame milk, but then I had to figure out how to get it to her. I knew she stopped at Morning Dove on her way to work twice a week. I ... might have followed her around for a while. I thought it would look too suspicious if I was the only one there, which is why I asked you guys to come along. It just seemed fitting to tell you about Martin's affair while we were there. Kind of ironic, you know? I was going to try to put the sesame creamers on her table before she got there, but I realized there was no guarantee that she would sit at the same table she usually did, so I decided to try to sneak the creamers in if she got up later. Valerie actually helped me out there without knowing it. I was going to try to come up with a reason to switch out the bowls myself, but she gave me the perfect excuse, and right as Mariah left her table, too."

"Oh, my gosh," Sierra breathed. "You actually did it. You actually killed her. Lydia was right when she thought one of us did it."

"No, I was wrong," Lydia said. "I thought it had something to do with the EpiPen."

Sierra frowned and looked at Taylor. "Did you do that too?"

"I kicked it out of the way when it fell," Taylor confirmed. "I dropped the purse on purpose. I didn't know if the EpiPen would save her life, and I had kind of forgotten about it until that point, so I had to think fast. I wanted to make sure she suffered for what she did."

"I can't believe this," Sierra said. "This can't be real. Please tell me the two of you came up with this as some sort of horrible prank."

"I'm sorry for involving you in this, but I don't regret it," Taylor said, crossing her arms. "She deserved what happened to her."

"You murdered someone, Taylor," Lydia said slowly. "Do you understand that?"

"Don't talk down to me like that, Lydia," Taylor said, lifting her chin. "Of course I understand the gravity of what I did. It's been keeping me up at night, but I still don't regret it. If anything, she deserved to suffer more. She knew exactly what she was doing, exactly who she was hurting, and she did it anyway."

Lydia shook her head, more out of disbelief than denial. Everything, all of this, the fights with her friends, all of her worries over her restaurant's policies surrounding allergies, all of Cynthia's self-recriminations... Taylor had watched them all go through it and hadn't said a word. And on top of that, she had *murdered* someone.

"I understand if the two of you don't agree with what I did," Taylor said when the silence stretched on. "But I hope you can at least understand why I did it. I don't want to lose you two as friends."

"Lose us as friends?" Lydia said hoarsely. "You're going to be in prison, Taylor. I think keeping us as friends should be your smallest concern right now."

"There's no way the police are going to figure out it was me," Taylor said. She paused. "You two are going to keep my secret, right?"

"Do you really think I'm going to cover up for murder?" Lydia asked, staring at Taylor. She had known this woman for years, but now she was beginning to wonder if she had ever known her at all.

Taylor looked at Sierra as if for help, and though Sierra looked both heartbroken and stunned, she shook her head. "I'm not going to help you get away with murder either, Taylor. I can't believe you did something like this."

Taylor rose to her feet slowly. "Seriously? You're going to tell the police about this? I could spend the rest of my life in prison."

Neither of them answered. Taylor backed away until she was near the table they had put their purses on. She grabbed them, rifling through the bags for their phones while they watched, both too stunned to move. Her hands shook as she held the cell phones up.

"I'm not going to give these back until we talk about this. You need some time to cool down."

Lydia glanced at Taylor's spot at the table. She had left her own cell phone sitting next to her plate. Taylor spotted it at the same time she did, but Lydia managed to grab it first. The phone was locked, but she didn't need to unlock it to make an emergency call.

"Please, Lydia, don't do this. Just think about it, we've been friends for so long. Doesn't that mean anything?"

Taylor continued to babble frantically as Sierra rose to her feet and gently pulled her away from Lydia. Sierra looked more torn than Lydia felt, but her expression was resolved. Lydia wasn't sure where they would go from here, but she knew she had lost Taylor as a friend even before she dialed 911.

Murder was one thing Lydia couldn't overlook.

EPILOGUE

"Volunteer work sucks."

Lydia looked sideways at her friend. They were walking through Quarry Creek, stopping in at each business they passed to ask if they could hang a flyer advertising Morning Dove's midwinter, week-long special prices. The café had been struggling ever since Mariah's death, and even the truth coming out hadn't helped. Lydia had been talking to Cynthia whenever she went in, and when the other woman asked her for help with the flyers, she hadn't hesitated to agree.

Sierra was out here with her because Lydia had plied her with free food from Iron and Flame before asking for her help. The idea was to make it go faster with two people passing out the fliers separately, but in reality, it was a lot more fun to walk down the icy sidewalk together, so they could chat in between talking to the business owners.

"Neither of us wants Morning Dove to close down," Lydia reminded her. "This is for the good of the community."

"I know you're right, but I'm still going to complain," Sierra said with a sigh. She hesitated, then added, "So … do you want to come with me to visit her?"

There was no question that she was talking about Taylor.

"I don't think I can," Lydia said. "It's too early. Definitely not now, maybe never. I know she didn't do anything to hurt me, not directly, but I feel so betrayed by what she did. The murder, but also the gaslighting. She acted like there was something wrong with me for being suspicious about Mariah's death, when she knew exactly what happened all along."

"Are you going to be upset if I visit her?"

Lydia shook her head. "The two of you were always closer to each other than you were to me." Sierra opened her mouth as if to object, but Lydia cut her off. "No, it's true. I was busy with the restaurant and Jeremy and everything else, and it just worked out that way. It's fine. I just mean to say, I understand if you need to talk to her."

"I need to get some closure. I don't think I'll ever really understand why she did what she did, but I'd like to try. I feel like I owe that to the person she used to be, you know?"

"I understand," Lydia said. "Let me know how it goes?"

"I will." Sierra gave her a weak smile. "Let's talk about something else. Like ... when are you going to finally ask Jude on a date?"

Lydia snorted, pushing her way into an antique shop. They were almost done with the small downtown strip, which was all they had signed up to do. Cynthia had promised them free hot chocolates and a slice of peppermint cheesecake when they finished, and she was looking forward to the snack.

"When I finally make up my mind on if I'm ready to start dating or not," she said. "Sometimes I think it would be nice to find someone, other times it sounds so exhausting."

"You haven't had enough good relationships in your life," Sierra determined as they walked up to the counter, their fliers in hand. "You're too used to the way things were with Jeremy. With the right guy, the relationship won't be exhausting at all. And I know you aren't sure if Jude's the right guy or not yet, but that's the point of dating, to figure it out. Neither of us are getting any younger, Lydia. If you don't seize the day, you might not get the chance tomorrow."

"I'm going to pretend that wasn't super ominous," Lydia said. "It sounds like good advice, though. I'll think about it, okay?"

Sierra grinned triumphantly. "That's all I ask ... for now. But if you wait too long, I'll steal your phone and ask him out to dinner on your behalf."

With that threat hanging in the air, they turned their attention back to their job. Lydia's fingers and ears were cold, her boots were wet, and her nose wouldn't stop dripping from the frigid air outside. One of her oldest friends had been arrested for murder, and she was apparently on the verge of losing control of her love life, but despite all of that, she was smiling, and that was something.

Printed in Great Britain
by Amazon